Davie's Wee Dog

Davie's Wee Dog

William MacKellar

Illustrated by Barry Wilkinson

COLLINS : ARMADA LIONS

First published by the McGraw–Hill Book Company Inc,
New York 1957, as 'Wee Joseph'

First published in Great Britain by
The Bodley Head, 1965

The Armada edition of *Davie's Wee Dog* was
published in 1970 by Wm. Collins Sons and Co Ltd,
14 St James's Place, London sw1

First published in Armada Lions 1974

© William MacKellar 1957

Illustrations © The Bodley Head 1965

Printed in Great Britain by
Richard Clay (The Chaucer Press), Ltd,
Bungay, Suffolk.

For my father, John MacKellar

Contents

1. Davie Buys a Dog

Davie's eyes popped in his head. A slow pounding came from under his blue wool jersey where his heart was. Again he looked into Mr Blaikie's face. And again he looked at the squirming little creature that the farmer held in his hands.

'And you want only sixpence for him?' he repeated.

'That's all, Davie Campbell,' the farmer said heartily. 'And a fine beast he is too.'

Davie felt his breath strangle in his throat. He put out his hands. The farmer placed the little dog between the cupped fingers. For a long moment Davie just stood, too filled with emotion to speak. Gently he eased his forefinger down the little dog's back. It was strange how thin and uneven the fur was. Still he was only a pup. That would explain it.

'Aye, it's the fine one he is,' Mr Blaikie said. 'The fine one indeed.' He winked slyly at the boy. 'I've been saving him for yourself, Davie Campbell.'

The boy nodded but did not answer. He had never liked Mr Blaikie very much. As a matter of fact he couldn't recall any one in the whole village of Stranmore ever having said anything kind about the farmer. Still it was good of him to have saved the little pup just for him. Just went to show how wrong people could be about other people sometimes.

Again Davie's finger trailed across the pup's skimpy coat. It was queer how many colours it had. Most dogs that Davie had seen had only two colours. *This* little pup— why, it was a rainbow of all kinds of hues— white and black and brown and russet and pink! Surely there had never been such a wonderfully coloured dog!

'Aye, it's the grand dog he is for certain, Mr Blaikie,' he agreed. 'Will you look at the rare markings on him? I'm thinking there will not be many like him in these parts.'

Mr Blaikie laughed as though Davie had just said something very funny. 'Aye, he's different, I'll say *that* for him. A rare kind as you rightly said, Davie Campbell.'

'And you want only sixpence for him, Mr Blaikie?'

The farmer nodded. His eyes, too close together, narrowed slightly. His face no longer wore its smile of good humour when he spoke.

'You've got the money?' he snapped. 'But of course you have! Or why would you be asking for the wee dog?' He stretched out his big hand and waited.

Davie hesitated. The sixpence in his pocket was a lot of money. It was everything he had—the sum of all his work for the past month. His father would be angry at first when he learned it had been spent. But when he caught sight of the wee dog, he would understand. Holding the pup in one hand, Davie dug his fingers into the pocket of his trousers. Slowly he withdrew the small silver coin and dropped it into the farmer's hand. Mr Blaikie's crafty face was all smiles again.

'Mind you take good care of him!' He chuckled as he turned away. 'There will not be many like him in these parts.'

Suddenly he laughed again, just as he had laughed before. Davie could see nothing funny in what he had said. Still, if Mr Blaikie

11

wanted to laugh that was *his* business. Anyway who cared? For a moment he watched as the farmer turned and walked away. Then his eyes went to the small bundle of uneven fur that lay cradled in his hands. A great joy rose like a hot flame in Davie Campbell. Tenderly he poked his finger under a round, pink nose. He was rewarded a moment later when a small red tongue curled out and took a solemn lick at his finger.

'Aye,' he said huskily. 'It's plain to see you're a grand dog. A grand dog, indeed!'

Again Davie ran his fingers admiringly over the pup's body. It was strange, though, how close the ribs seemed to be against the coat; almost as if there were no flesh at all on the wee body, as if the pup had been starved. But who would ever starve a fine dog like this now? Davie dismissed the thought at once.

'I'll call you Joseph,' he said suddenly, and knew that of all names, *this* was the right one. For hadn't they just read last week in Sunday school about Joseph and his coat of many colours?

'Joseph,' he said softly. 'I'm talking to you, Joseph.'

The freckled nose wrinkled. A gangling ear twitched ever so slightly. A moist brown eye winked open.

'He knows his name already,' marvelled Davie. Pride made the words tight in his throat.

2. Mr Leckie Disapproves

The scent of the bog myrtle rode the soft hill wind and moved with a slow sweetness in Davie's nostrils. Joseph lay crooked in his arms as he started the journey back to his home. Davie's bare feet moved easily through the coarse, dry heather. When first he had doffed his shoes with the coming of the warm June days, the bracken fronds and the spiky heather shoots had seemed harsh against his feet. Now he could take even the thorniest undergrowth in stride. He hummed as he walked.

'Good day to you, Davie,' a man called from a small granite house with trim green shutters.

'Good day to you, Mr Leckie,' Davie said to the schoolmaster.

The teacher leaned on the gate leading to his garden and smiled.

'What do you have there, Davie?'

Davie smiled back proudly. 'A dog,

Mr Leckie. And it's a fine dog he is too!'

'H-m.' Mr Leckie's lips pursed slightly as he looked at the dog. 'Where did you get him, Davie?'

'From Mr Blaikie.' He stopped. He knew there was something else he should say. 'For sixpence.'

'For sixpence?' A shadow fell across the schoolteacher's face. 'May I look at him, Davie?'

Carefully the boy handed the dog over. 'His name's Joseph.'

'H-m.' Again Mr Leckie's lips set in a tight line. His long fingers moved slowly over the dog. The shadow darkened on his face.

'You paid sixpence for him, you said?'

'Aye.'

'I see.' With a little grunt the schoolmaster returned the dog to the boy. 'I'm afraid our Mr Blaikie is as big a rascal as people say he is.'

Davie stopped, his hands around Joseph. 'What do you mean?'

'Just that this Joseph of yours isn't quite the fine dog Mr Blaikie claimed he was.'

Davie stared, then leaped to defend Joseph. 'Are you saying he's not got the grand blood at all?'

The schoolmaster let his hand drop gently on Davie's shoulder. 'I'm afraid he's just a mongrel, Davie. This dog was evidently one of a large litter. The mother couldn't take care of him. Mr Blaikie didn't bother. Why just look at the poor thing, Davie! He's skin and bones!'

'But he's only a wee pup,' Davie protested. 'Besides, why should Mr Blaikie see that the other pups were fed and not Joseph?'

Mr Leckie sighed. 'Tastes in dogs differ, Davie. Your taste is the right one for you. However, most people wouldn't like Joseph. All his markings are in the wrong places. And he's got the oddest colours I've ever seen. Besides, his legs are too short and his body is too long and his ears don't match. Why, you'd think they had been meant for two different dogs.' He shook his head sadly. 'I'm afraid, Davie,' he said, 'most people would call Joseph a misfit.'

'A mis . . .?' Davie clamped his jaws tight to contain the bitter word. Not Joseph! His blue eyes blazed fiercely as he backed away from the schoolteacher and held Joseph in his arms.

'As you said before, Mr Leckie, it's a matter

17

of taste. Good day to you.' Quickly he turned away.

Mr Leckie called after him. 'Good day to you too, Davie.'

What was the matter with the man, thought Davie angrily. Aye, and him a schoolteacher too! Calling Joseph a misfit! It was a wonder Joseph hadn't leaped at his throat. Aye, a wonder indeed! He lifted his arms and held his face close to Joseph. He could feel the soft warmth steal up from the pup's body. The coarse hair moved ever so gently against Davie's cheek in time with the scrawny little creature's breathing.

Joseph was fast asleep.

3. Enter Tam Menzies

Davie had stopped to rest by a mossy dike, smothered in a net of white hawthorns, when Joseph stirred and woke. Gently the boy placed the pup down on the ground. He watched with delight from his rocky perch as Joseph moved through the long grass.

Actually he didn't move *through* the grass as much as he moved *over* it. It may have been because of his short legs or his lack of strength to bend back the tough reeds. Or perhaps it was just that Joseph wanted to see where he was going. *That* was it, thought Davie. He sat on the dike, his bare feet dangling, and followed Joseph's freckled nose rising and falling through the thick grass and heather. Finally, Joseph trotted back to where Davie sat.

After halting by a small spring and swallowing the tooth-numbing cold water, they continued on their way. The ground was rough and thick with briars and bramble bushes. Davie took the pup in his arms. They had still a number of miles to go before they reached home. He sang as he walked, for he had forgotten all about Mr Leckie.

Will ye no come back again,
Will ye no, Prince Charlie?
Better loved ye canna be,
Will ye no come back again?

Why he should sing of Bonnie Prince Charlie was hard to say. It was just that, with Joseph in his arms, it *seemed* only right to sing. And when your heart puts a song on your lips you don't argue. You just sing. So Davie sang.

Better loved ye canna be,
Will ye no come back again?

Of course it was true that after the battle on Culloden Moor Bonnie Prince Charlie had hidden in this very glen. Every schoolboy in the village knew the story—how the Prince had fled in the night with the Duke of Cumberland's soldiers at his heels and had lain hidden all night in the cold mists of Ben Ulva, the huge mountain at the head of the glen. With the morning light the Prince had escaped to the Hebrides.

Ben Ulva still sat at the head of the glen, looking like a huge whale trapped in a fine net of silvery mist. Yet it was no longer the same mountain that the last of the Stuarts had looked at. Progress had come to the Highlands. A thin line of metal pylons marched in single file up the mountain. Davie could see the workmen, in the distance like tiny ants busy at their tasks. He knew what these tasks were. The Government had decided to open up the Highlands—to tame the wild rivers and the floods, to bring cheap power and electricity. Life would be easier for all.

Davie had just swung over the crest of the small hill when he heard the shrill skirl. So suddenly did it come that for a moment he felt the blood turn cold in his veins. Then he smiled. Of course! Old Tam Menzies, the hermit. Tam lived on the farm over the hill. Everyone thought he was crazy, but Davie knew better. Tam just thought things out differently.

The high thin skirl of the bagpipes drew

nearer. Then from behind a screen of pine trees stepped an old man. His hair was a long white train in the wind. His cheeks as he puffed were two bright red apples. He paused when he saw Davie, and the air in the chanter and drones of the pipes choked and became still.

'A good day to you, Davie Campbell,' he said in a high-pitched voice.

'A good day to you, Mr Menzies,' Davie returned civilly.

The hermit stood on tiptoe and craned his neck forward.

'What have you got there, Davie lad?' he cried shrilly. 'There's something hidden in that hand of yours. I'll bet a shilling on it.' His little eyes seemed to climb over Davie's hand.

'A dog.'

'A dog, no less?'

'Aye.'

The old hermit's face wrinkled with pleasure. Tenderly he took the pup from Davie. He parted the floppy ears and tickled Joseph's head.

'My!' he breathed, his eyes aglow. 'Is he not the grand wee dog?'

'He is that!' Davie acknowledged proudly. He smiled with his eyes at the hermit. What a knowing old man he was! And yet they called him crazy!

'A fine dog he is, eh, Davie? Aye, but that's for certain. It's plain to see there's the grand blood in him.'

Davie's red head bobbed in quick agreement. 'Aye, for certain.' How clever of the old man to have spotted Joseph's worth so quickly! Suddenly he remembered Mr Leckie, remembered the cruel things that he had said. The boy looked open-faced at his friend. If anybody knew, it would be Tam Menzies.

'And how can you tell for certain, Mr Menzies?' he asked anxiously.

'Eh? Tell what, lad?'

'That there's the grand blood in him?'

'Oh, that now.' The hermit scratched his long nose thoughtfully. He whistled between his thin lips. He frowned. He turned Joseph carefully over and squinted through one eye at him. Then he laughed merrily. He dug a bony finger playfully into Davie's ribs.

'How can you tell what's a rowan tree and what's not a rowan tree? Answer me that, Davie Campbell.'

24

The boy frowned. He had seen hundreds of rowan trees. He recognized them as soon as he saw them. But how did he know for certain? Somehow the old man's question wasn't so easy to answer as it seemed.

'I'm not sure at all, Mr Menzies,' he said truthfully. 'It's just that somehow a rowan tree *looks* like what a rowan tree should be.'

'Right!' squealed old Tam triumphantly. 'And that's the same with the wee dog here! He looks like a dog would look that had the grand blood in him. And what better proof will you be wanting, lad, than that?' The hermit's pale blue eyes seemed to be doing a Highland fling of delight in his head. Old Tam prided himself on his logic.

Davie took back Joseph and set him on the ground. How right he had been about old Tam Menzies! Crazy? Why, there was no one sharper in all Scotland!

When they had gone a few hundred yards along, Davie turned and looked back and waved. Old Tam Menzies was standing on a rock. The wind made a halo of his white hair. He raised a thin bony arm in farewell. Then he lifted the blowpipe to his lips. The high skirl of the pipes carried faintly to Davie's ears across the glen.

The boy turned again and waved back gratefully to his friend. Old Tam Menzies crazy? Why, he didn't even *look* crazy.

4. Waiting in the Cottage

Nell Campbell looked at her son. There was surprise in her eyes. There was pain there too, but Davie didn't see it.

'A dog, Davie?' she said. She stared at the little creature with the queer blotches of colour.

'Aye. I got him from Mr Blaikie for sixpence.'

'For sixpence?'

He looked up quickly, sensing the distress in her voice. 'He's worth it—aye, and more,' he said stoutly. He watched as Joseph greedily sank his tongue into the saucer of milk. The puppy made queer little slurpings of pleasure as his tongue scooped up the milk.

'His name's Joseph,' Davie said when his mother didn't speak.

'Joseph?'

'Aye, like him in the Bible. The one with the coat with all the colours.'

She smiled just a little sadly. Her fingers

were a familiar softness on Davie's red hair, like no other softness in all the world.

'Davie, Davie,' she murmured, her face very close to his. 'In many ways he was not a very happy man, that Joseph of yours. I'm thinking your wee dog is too well named.'

He felt her fingers tighten on his shoulder. He looked up and could feel the sudden coldness that cramped his stomach.

'And why?' he said. Although now he knew with a terrible sureness what the answer would be.

'Your father, Davie.' She rushed on lest he should misunderstand. 'It's a just man he is, and kind in many ways, Davie. In ways you're too young to know. But he fights hard to put the bread in our mouths. And he can't abide the vanities of the world.'

'Vanities?' cried Davie, pointing his finger at Joseph. 'You call Joseph a vanity?'

She let the little smile have its way with her mouth. 'Joseph is a fine wee dog. But we'll not be able to use him. And if we'll not be able to use him, I'm afraid'—her voice sank to a whisper—'we'll not be able to keep him.' She paused. 'I'm sorry, Davie.'

He did not answer. What answer was there

to give? Or what meaning could there be in any answer? It was his father who would say what should be. Or what should not be. His father, that tall dark man with the stern eyes and the sterner mouth. The sombre man who worked from early dawn to sunset to scrape a living from the flinty soil. Ian Campbell was not a man who smiled often. Or often had much to smile about.

Davie sat in the kitchen with Joseph and waited. He had given the dog a few scraps of meat and made a little bed of rags and straw for him. Into this Joseph had climbed and, curling up in a ball, had fallen fast asleep.

The hours passed slowly. Davie's mother worked quietly in the light by the window, her needle moving swiftly, endlessly. With the late afternoon sun glinting on the mirror over the big dresser, she rose to get the supper ready. The heavy smell of the bubbling pot of broth steamed the room. A griddle of scones hung over the ruddy peat fire.

She did not speak to Davie. Davie did not speak to her. Other than her movements the only sound in the kitchen was the *ticktock*, *ticktock* of the old wall clock.

The shadows lengthened in the room. The flames became brighter in the hearth. The tiny dust whorls no longer slid down the slanting rays of sunlight. The gloom seemed a living thing—a great evil fog creeping into every nook and cranny—until finally there was no hiding place. Not even in a small boy's heart.

The oil lamp on the table had just been lit when Davie's brothers, Murdoch and Jimmy, came in. Murdoch and Jimmy were men. Murdoch, long-jawed and dark, was eighteen. Jimmy, square-faced and fair, was sixteen. They stared in amazement when they spotted the dog.

'Am I dreaming!' Murdoch exclaimed. He pointed a big finger. 'What's that?'

Davie was on his feet between Murdoch and the dog. '*That* is Joseph,' he said defiantly. 'And he's mine.'

There was a sudden silence. A fire-charred peat fell with a slushing sound into the ashes at the bottom of the grate. 'Yours?' Murdoch asked.

'Aye.'

'And does your father know this?' It was Jimmy who asked the question.

Ever so slightly Davie moved his head. 'No.'

'Ah!' The older brothers seemed to say it together. Their eyes met and Jimmy laughed a little nervously and patted Davie roughly on the head.

'Good luck to you, Davie,' he said simply.

Murdoch grunted but said nothing. Yet from time to time his eyes travelled slowly to Joseph and then to Davie. Once he shook his head.

The light from the oil lamp flickered in the kitchen. Little puddles of brightness splashed up and down the pine-panelled wall. Jimmy whistled off key as he washed. Jimmy never whistled before eating. His whistling sounded strange in Davie's ears.

Suddenly Jimmy's pursed lips froze. The air between his teeth was still. He cocked his head towards the door. But Davie had already heard. Heard the heavy sound of the foot on the gravel outside the door. He felt his heartbeat grow big in his chest. His father had come home!

The door opened and the cold night air rushed in. Then Ian Campbell entered. He stood there for a long moment, his big

shoulders bowed, his deep-set eyes bleak with weariness. Then he looked up and saw Joseph. He stopped where he was.

'What is this?' he said. He closed the door behind him.

5. Ian Campbell Meets Joseph

'Now, Ian,' Nell Campbell said with a show of brightness, 'there's no reason at all to look so surprised. It's just a wee dog that Davie brought home.'

'We have no room for dogs here,' Ian Campbell said. 'Nor food either, I'm thinking.' He shrugged off his work jacket and tossed it over a straight-backed chair. He frowned at Joseph, asleep in his box.

'Where did you get this beast, Davie?' he asked calmly.

He did not look angry. Encouraged, Davie told the story of how he had got Joseph from Mr Blaikie. At first he had meant to hide the fact that he had paid for him. Now, with Joseph's worth at stake, he thought it best to mention the sixpence that the dog cost him.

'Aye, but he's worth it, he is,' the boy finished. 'For he's a fine dog!' He stopped, knowing there should be something else he

35

should say. 'Aye, and it's the great help he'll be around the house.'

The silence was thick in the kitchen. It seemed to drip from the very beams in the ceiling. Then it was torn asunder by the sound of his father's voice.

'You paid sixpence for the like of that! Hard-earned money thrown away sinfully to a rogue and thief like Blaikie! Could you not have seen that the dog is worthless?'

The voice was a terrible loudness in Davie's ears. It was hard to think. There was a queer spinning and tumbling in his mind, and it was impossible to sort the words out. The words that needed to be spoken if Joseph were to stay.

'Have you no tongue?' Ian Campbell said.

'He's not worthless! I don't care what you think!' And now that the words were there, the courage was there too. He looked with defiance at this man whom he feared and was beginning to hate. 'There's the grand blood in him. Mr Blaikie said so. Aye, and so did old Tam Menzies!'

Little points of light stabbed at the darkness in Ian Campbell's eyes. For a moment his big hand went up and Davie felt a quick weakness in his legs as he waited for the blow to fall. But no blow fell. Davie blinked his eyes open.

'It is well for you, Davie, that I am slow to anger,' Ian Campbell said between thin lips. He breathed deeply, and his outgoing breath was a soft rasp in the heavy air. 'I am not in the habit of reasoning with my sons. Yet I would not want you to think I am unjust.' He stopped and closed his eyes with a quick tiredness. 'I am a very just man, Davie.'

'Then be just with Joseph here!' Davie pleaded.

Ian Campbell nodded. His dark face was calm again. The sudden tiredness gone. He pointed to a chair. 'Do you see that chair, Davie?'

He nodded. 'Aye.'

'And what will it be for?'

'To sit on.'

'And those shoes under the bed?'

'To put on your feet.'

'And that plate, Davie?'

'To eat from.'

Ian Campbell stopped. 'They all have a purpose, eh?'

'Aye.'

'They all have a use?'

'Aye.'

Ian Campbell's long finger stabbed forward and pointed straight at Joseph. 'And what of that miserable beast? What purpose—aye, what use is *he*?' His voice cracked like a lash, and Davie flinched.

'He—he——' the boy floundered. He tried hard to think of something to say on Joseph's behalf. Somehow Joseph didn't have any purpose, really. Except maybe to make the world a little brighter by just being in it.

'I'm waiting, Davie.'

He looked again at the dog. 'I just like him,' he said gravely. Somehow there didn't seem to be anything more one could add to that.

'Vain affection!' thundered Ian Campbell. His brow was black. 'This is no useful dog! It's but a cur for preening and sinful pampering! Our bread is hard earned, Davie Campbell. I will not have it used to feed a useless beast. Do you hear that?'

'Aye,' he said. His voice was a small dryness in his throat. He did not look at his father.

'Good,' Ian Campbell said grimly. He

paused, then said with a quick mildness, 'You can keep him here for the night. There will be no harm in it.'

Davie did not answer. There was nothing to say. Joseph still slept. What was it his mother had said? *'In many ways he was not a very happy man, that Joseph of yours. I'm thinking your wee dog was too well named.'*

His mother was right, of course. Joseph hadn't been the happiest of men. With his coat of many colours he had been sold into slavery. He had known hunger. He had known loneliness. He had been in prison. Yet in the end everything had worked out well.

Somehow the thought was a slight comfort to Davie as he took his place at the table.

6. Davie Gets His Orders

While Murdoch and Jimmy exchanged small talk at the table, Nell Campbell poured out the bowls of steaming broth. She sliced the bread that she had made the day before and gave Davie the half with the white crust that he loved so much. Usually he would dip it into the broth until it was soggy. Then, while it still dripped barley and leeks and peas he would let his teeth sink into the warm, sweet softness. But tonight Davie let the bread lie where it was.

When the tea was poured, Davie's mother put the scones and oatcakes on the table. Davie nibbled moodily at the oatcake. The nutty paste was coarse against his tongue as the cake crumbled and melted in his mouth. Around him he heard the voices of the others. They seemed remote and distant. Once Jimmy laughed. Then the dishes were gathered up and the family pulled itself into a tight semicircle around the blazing fireplace.

'You can give the dog a bit of the meat, Davie, if you've a mind to,' Ian Campbell said as he sank into the ancient leather arm-chair.

Davie, who had already hidden away several choice pieces, did not reply. He cut up the food into tiny pieces and placed them in a clean tin saucer. He watched as Joseph's little jaws busily set to work. The dog was hungry and licked the saucer clean in a matter of seconds. Davie gave him a little more meat, then, fearful that his father might think that Joseph ate like this *all* the time, set a dish of water before him. Joseph drank noisily, his long ears just missing the water.

After a while Ian Campbell laid down the book he was reading. His mind seemed far away as he gazed fixedly at the dancing flames in the hearth.

'Tomorrow, Davie, you will take the beast back to Mr Blaikie. You will ask him for the sixpence. It's not in his nature to give it back, I'm thinking. Be that as it will, you will still return the wee dog to him. Is that clear?'

'Aye.' Davie's voice was low. He pulled his hand gently back and forth across Joseph's

skimpy coat. The dog seemed to tremble and whimper and draw closer to Davie's hand. *He knows*, thought Davie. He was suddenly aware that his father was still speaking.

'—and if Mr Blaikie will not give you the sixpence and will not take the dog back, then you had better see that someone else gets him. For, mark my words, Davie, this dog has no place in this house. *No* place. Do you understand that?'

Davie's lips twitched just enough to let the word out. 'Aye.'

'Good.' Ian Campbell's eyes returned to the book in his hands.

While Jimmy chattered and laughed and Murdoch worked over a split bamboo salmon rod the evening slid quietly away. Nell Campbell's needle rose and fell, rose and fell. Joseph, after sniffing his way around the kitchen a few times, made his way back to where Davie lay on the floor. Ian Campbell read. The peats changed colour in the fireplace. The little tide of ashes lapped higher in the hearth.

Suddenly Ian Campbell closed his book. He pressed his big hands against the arms of the chair and eased himself to his feet. His bulk cut across the light from the fireplace. The shadow fell directly on where Joseph lay curled up on the floor.

Davie felt the quick coldness press against his heart, almost as though a door had suddenly opened and let in the night air. His father's rising from his chair meant only one thing. The day had come to an end.

Davie got to his feet. It was time for bed. The day was over. This was the day that had brought Joseph to him. Now it was finished. When he woke in the morning there would be a new day waiting—a day that would take Joseph away from him.

7. No Home for Joseph

Mr Blaikie laughed, a high shrill laugh without any humour in it.

'On your way, Davie Campbell!' he cried. 'The wee dog is yours, fairly sold and fairly bought.'

'It's not just the sixpence,' Davie said. 'My father said you can keep the sixpence. He—he says you should keep Joseph, too.'

'Keep him?' The farmer laughed again. When he laughed the suety flesh moved in his face and seemed to bury the small, darting eyes. 'What kind of a fool do you think I am, Davie Campbell? Waste honest food on a thing like *that*!' He pointed a scornful finger at Joseph.

Davie stared. 'But didn't you say yourself he was a fine dog?'

The farmer chuckled deep in his throat. He pushed Davie forward with a rough hand. 'Now get along with you! There's work to be done.'

Davie fell back a few steps. All at once he felt the quick fear that crept up his spine on cold rat feet. If Mr Blaikie wouldn't take the pup for *nothing* what would become of Joseph? Suppose *everybody* in Stranmore felt the same way? Davie watched as Mr Blaikie turned and went back to his farm. It just couldn't be! Somebody would surely want Joseph!

It was not until two full hours later, after

having knocked at every door in Stranmore, that he finally realized that *nobody* wanted Joseph. It was not that most of the people weren't kind. They were. And it wasn't that some of them weren't looking for a dog. They were. It was just that when they saw Joseph they seemed to lose interest. A few had even laughed, and asked where on earth he had ever got such a dog. But in the end the result was always the same. Nobody wanted Joseph.

Davie walked away from the village with Joseph at his heels. He followed his feet blindly through the rough country. Hot tears scalded his eyes at the corners. Finally he reached a small hollow behind a row of scrawny pine trees. He flung himself forward and buried his face in the tall grass. Small sobs shook his shoulders.

After a while he stirred and drew an angry sleeve across his eyes. This was no time for crying. It was a time for thinking —for thinking what to do about Joseph. The little dog lay panting by his feet, his mouth open, his small pink tongue showing.

'There's got to be a way, Joseph, there's just got to!' he whispered.

He closed his eyes in an effort to think more clearly. It was strange how when one shut one's eyes, one's ears seemed to open. As he lay on his stomach he could hear the wind whisper through the blades of grass. The lazy hum of the bees drowsing among the clover carried to his ears. From far away came the peevish cry of a lapwing. And then suddenly there was another sound, high and shrill, and then a cackle of laughter.

'If it's not Davie Campbell himself, and his bonnie wee dog.'

Davie blinked his eyes open. It was old Tam Menzies.

8. Of Faith and Mustard Seeds

The hermit listened, bright-eyed and solemn as Davie told his story. From time to time the old man tugged at his ear as though in deep thought. He scratched his head when Davie had finished.

'A hard problem you give me, Davie.'

'Aye, but are you not the clever one, Mr Menzies?' Davie pointed out. 'Are you forgetting that?'

'True, true,' the hermit said quickly. 'I have a rare cleverness. I'm glad you reminded me of it.' He frowned again and tugged nervously at his long, crooked nose. Suddenly his gentle eyes brightened.

'I've got it, laddie! I'll take the wee dog! Then you can come and see him whenever you've a mind to!' He wheezed with pleasure. 'How will *that* be for clever thinking, Davie Campbell?'

The boy was just about to let out a whoop

of delight when he remembered something. He shook his head slightly.

'I'm afraid my father will not let you have Joseph,' he said. He didn't quite know how to go on without hurting his old friend. 'He—he'll not be knowing you as well as I do.'

Tam Menzies nodded. 'Aye, he'll be thinking I'm daft, is that it, Davie?'

'Aye.' He did not look at the hermit.

'But you don't think I'm daft, now, do you?'

The boy shook his head. 'I think you are the clever one for certain. In all Stranmore it was only you that saw the grand blood in Joseph.'

'Aye, that was clever of Tam Menzies, was it not?' the old man said, pleased.

'Anyway,' said Davie with a frown, 'we've got to think of something.'

'I just *thought* of something,' the old man pointed out, a slightly hurt look on his face. 'Now you want me to think again.'

'Sorry.'

'It's not easy to think clever twice in a row,' grumbled the hermit.

'Even once in a row is hard,' Davie said politely.

'Aye, it is that. Even for Tam Menzies. Now let me see, Davie, let me see.' His frown seemed to tug his whole face out of shape. Suddenly his long fingers cracked.

'I've done it again, Davie!' he croaked in triumph. 'I've thought clever twice in a row!' He laughed shrilly and clapped his hands in glee.

'What is the clever thought this time?' Davie asked eagerly.

The old man grinned. 'Find the mustard seed.'

Davie stared. For one moment he almost was afraid his old friend *was* crazy.

'Find the what, Mr Menzies?'

'Mustard seed. Mustard seed,' the hermit said a little crossly. 'I read about it a long time ago in the Bible. It says if you have faith like a grain of mustard seed, you can do anything. Aye, even move mountains.' He scowled and scratched his head. 'Now tell me this, Davie Campbell, what sane man would want to go around moving mountains?'

'I don't know,' Davie said frankly. It *did* seem an odd sort of pastime. He frowned and looked at the hermit. 'And where will I find the mustard seed, Mr Menzies?'

Old Tam sighed. He moved his head and shook his finger gently at the boy. 'It all comes from asking hard questions, Davie. We had it all taken care of just fine. Then you had to ask where you could find the mustard seed. That was the hard question that spoiled everything.'

'I'm sorry,' the boy said miserably.

'Never ask hard questions, Davie Campbell. Then if you don't get the right answer, you don't feel so bad.'

Davie nodded. It seemed to make sense. He was sorry he had asked Mr Menzies the hard question. Still, if he hadn't, how was he ever going to find the mustard seed that seemed to matter so much? It was all very confusing.

With Joseph romping at his heels, he made his way home, his mind an overturned bee-hive of quick, humming thoughts. Everyone thought the old hermit with the long white beard was crazy. But he knew differently. Menzies was smart. Smart as a whip. Who else could have thought of saving Joseph with faith and mustard seeds? True, he had yet to find the mustard seed, but if he had faith he could.

He stopped. Faith? Somehow he had taken that part of it too much for granted.

He was just about to ask himself whether he had faith to believe that everything would be all right with Joseph. Then he remembered. Remembered what old Tam Menzies had said. Quickly he shook the thought from his mind.

Better not to ask any hard questions. Even of one's self. No telling what kind of answer he might get.

9. A Prayer for Joseph

Ian Campbell said grimly, 'So you failed even to give the beast away, eh, Davie?'

'Tam Menzies wanted him,' the boy said. He took his courage in his hands and looked straight at his father. 'And I want him myself.'

'Silence!' thundered Ian Campbell. With an effort he seemed to gain control of himself. Yet his voice was brittle with passion when he resumed.

'You are my son. You will do what you are told. When you are told. That beast is useless. I have already told you so. No one will take it. Even for nothing. No one except old Tam Menzies. And Christian that I am, I would turn no defenceless creature of God's over to a poor daft man.'

Davie looked at him, the misery in his eyes blurring his vision so that he could make out only the form of his father and a grim, harsh mouth. The words that he spoke were a thickness against his tongue, a strangeness in his ears.

'And if I'm not to keep Joseph and if there's no one to take him, what's to become of him?'

Ian Campbell hesitated. When he spoke, he spoke softly, almost gently. 'To set a poor wee beast loose in the hills would be cruel.' He looked at his son. 'We are not cruel, are we, Davie?'

The boy swallowed. 'No,' he said.

Ian Campbell nodded approval. 'I'm glad you understand that, lad. I would not want you to think I'm a hard man.'

Davie waited, silent.

'What's left for me to do, then, is best for the dog.' The big hands spread out in a gesture of helplessness. 'Best for the dog, aye, and everyone.'

'Best for——' Davie looked up quickly. The sudden sickness in his body made his legs tremble.

'Tomorrow,' said Ian Campbell quietly, 'I will take the dog up to the Angus River. And I will come home alone.'

'No!' Davie cried. 'You won't! You won't!'

'I won't?' Ian Campbell's face darkened.

'I'll take him myself.' He hadn't meant to say it, but now that it was said, it was better said. 'I'll take him myself,' he said again, only quieter this time.

'I see.' The grimness was still there on his father's face. 'So that we understand each other, what will you do in the morning?'

Davie did not look at him.

'I'll take him up—up——' His whisper collapsed under its burden of grief and when he opened his mouth there were no words there.

'To the hills,' prodded Ian Campbell.

'To the hills,' Davie repeated.

The eyes, bleak as mist, remained fixed on the boy.

'And place him in the river.'

'And place him'—he swallowed—'in the river.'

'Good.' The matter settled, Ian Campbell picked up a book and eased himself into his chair by the fire. He read in silence, his lips moving slightly as his eyes travelled across the fine lines of print. He seemed to have forgotten his son. Yet when he finally rose to go to his room he hesitated by the door, then called to Davie over his shoulder.

'I am a just man, Davie, as you know. And

sometimes what we *must* do is not easy at all.'
He paused and sighed a little and it was as
though all the great strength in him had been
used up, for there was a quietness in his voice
when he spoke. 'Good night to you, Davie
lad.'

Davie did not answer. The hatred in his
heart for his father was a searing flame.
Hatred for the cold eyes and the colder words.
Hatred for this justice which he preached.
Hatred for his world of useful things. A world
wide enough to include shoes and plates and
chairs and too narrow to hold a little dog.

He stumbled over to where Joseph lay in
his box. The puppy wound a pink tongue
around his finger as he lifted him up. And
when Davie crept into bed, he took the dog
with him and held him close in his arms.

He tried not to cry, but there was a queer
stinging behind his eyes and when the tears
came it felt better. And anyway if he cried a
little, who cared, for the room was dark and
no one could see. Except God, he reminded
himself. And God didn't seem to care. Or did
He?

His mind went back to his talk with old
Tam Menzies. He was sorry there seemed no

way to find the mustard seed. But surely if he just prayed, God would understand. Maybe that was where the faith came in. Maybe the thing that had moved the mountains had been the faith and not the mustard seed. Yes, that was it.

He never knew where the words came from but they were there on his lips and he spoke them.

'Oh Lord, I'm not asking You to move any mountains at all, unless it's Yourself has a mind to. And I'm not praying for Davie Campbell either. It's just wee Joseph here I'm thinking about. For he's got nobody at all but the both of us—You, Lord, and me, and I'm no help at all, at all. And oh, I know how busy You are what with one thing and another and the world the way it is. But I thought, Lord, that Joseph being such a wee dog maybe You could spare a wee miracle. For it's a miracle he'll be needing if he's going to live. Aye, and we'll be thanking You greatly for it, will Joseph and me.'

Sleep came late to Davie but it came finally, came in a great rolling tide of mist. And it gathered Davie up in its arms gently and lovingly, just as Davie had gathered Joseph up in his and bore him off to a land of dreamless peace.

10. Journey for Two

There was a small canvas bag near Davie's bed when he awoke. He did not have to ask who had left it, or what it was for. He tried not to look at it as he forced down the steaming plate of porridge that his mother gave him. The oatmeal, usually so smooth, seemed coarse against his tongue. Even the cold milk seemed flat and without taste.

When his mother's back was turned, he stole out of the kitchen with Joseph. He sensed that this morning his mother would have kissed him. And had she done so, there was no saying what he might do. Why, he might even break out into tears!

Her back was still turned as he started to draw the door closed. He looked at her with eyes swimming with love and hurt. And then just as he stood there with his hand on the knob Joseph let out a small whinny of impatience. Davie froze. He waited for his mother to swing around and discover him.

But she did not turn. Made no sign that she had ever heard. But she *must* have heard! It was only as he silently drew the door closed that he understood. His mother had read his heart. Had guessed at the tears behind his eyes. At his need to be alone. It was no accident that her back had been turned. No accident that she had not heard Joseph's whimper. And the tears that she did not see were bright in his eyes as he closed the door and slipped away from the cottage.

When Davie had arisen to find his father gone, his last hope to save Joseph had vanished. For how was Joseph to be spared if his father did not give the word? Now all that lay ahead was the bitter trip up the hills to where the Angus River flowed. Only that and a certain task that made his heart sick to think about.

It had rained during the night, but with the morning the skies had cleared. As they passed under the giant sycamore outside the house the breeze from the hills sent a gentle spray of moisture down on the boy and the dog. Joseph shook himself and sniffed his annoyance. Little drops of rain dripped down his nose like tears.

Davie walked slowly. The wetness from the ferns was a coolness between his toes, but he did not feel it. The air was fragrant with the scent of meadowsweet and clover. He drew no pleasure from it. At the head of the glen Ben Ulva had doffed its nightcap of sullen cloud and now wore a rose-pink bonnet. Davie didn't even look at it.

Once Joseph sighted a rabbit and went off in instant chase. The rabbit outdistanced him in a matter of seconds. To Joseph, though, the whole thing was a mighty triumph. He trotted back to Davie, his long ears swaying gently like the sporran on a Highlander's kilt. It was his first victory over the enemy. Unless there were rabbits waiting to be chased in heaven, it might well be his last.

As they approached the steep incline Davie felt his feet suddenly drag in the heather. He knew, with a terrible sureness, what lay beyond it. A frothing tumbling rush of peat-stained water. The Angus River.

Davie had almost reached the top of the steep hill when he noticed it. The stillness. The queer silence that made the hum of a bee loud in his ears. He stopped, wondering. Something was wrong. Was different. A solitary curlew flew past, trailing its mournful cry behind it. But that was all. Something was missing. Something familiar was gone. Something that belonged here. Then all at once in the sudden silence that closed in after the curlew's cry he knew what it was. He could not hear the Angus!

With a few quick bounds he crested the hill. He stopped short. The breath froze in his lungs at the sight that awaited him.

As far as his eyes could see the river was gone!

11. The Miracle

He stood for almost ten seconds where he was, his mind refusing to accept what his eyes beheld. It was impossible! The Angus had always been there. Had been there since time began. It was a part of the world itself. Like the sun and the moon and the stars. Its cheery gossip greeted every dawn. Its soft lullaby put every day to bed.

Slowly, as the shock grew less, Davie noticed other things. Although the river was gone, a deep brown channel remained, a channel of still pools and smooth flat rocks. Of long green reeds bending in chocolate-coloured mud. Of hundreds of round, white pebbles that gleamed in the sun.

'It's not to be believed at all,' he whispered in awe. Like one in a trance he walked across the bed of the river. The soft mud was a gentle coolness against his bare feet. It must have been like this, he thought, when Moses walked across the Red Sea with the Children of Israel. Only then the waters had been rolled back. Here they had been dried up.

Yet of one thing he was certain. God had heard his prayer after all. And he had answered it. True, it *was* a little strange that he had gone to so much trouble to save one little dog's life. But who can tell about prayers anyway?

He watched as Joseph dashed at full speed through the small puddles in the river bed. His skinny little legs seemed to falter as the water broke against him. The next second he would burst through and strut proudly back to Davie, his tail like a battle standard, his small whiskers coated with glistening drops of moisture.

Davie's heart was light. He had put Joseph into the river just as he had been ordered. He had not disobeyed his father. And Joseph was alive—alive—alive!

He sang as he went home, and he noticed how the world had changed. How dreary it had seemed as he had made his way to the Angus. It couldn't just be the sun, for the sun had been shining before. Only now, somehow, it shone *differently*. With a new warmth and friendliness. It couldn't be the soft wind that

smelled so sweet in his lungs. The wind had been there before. Only like the sun it was *different* now. The whole world was different now, full of rich gay colours and happy, happy tunes. And as Joseph sported gaily at his heels the song that he had sung that first day came to his lips.

Will ye no come back again,
Will ye no, Prince Charlie?
Better loved ye canna be,
Will ye no come back again?

And if Bonnie Prince Charlie had 'no come back again', at least Joseph had. Back to the world of warm suns and soft hill winds. Back to the world of rabbits to be chased and bones to be buried and ears to be scratched.

Suddenly Davie stopped his whistling. There was something else Joseph was coming back to. Something dark and chilling and fearful.

The world of Ian Campbell.

12. The Grand Blood

Ian Campbell stopped when he saw Davie and Joseph. With a big hand he swung the gate closed. With the other he set the wooden milk bucket down hard on the cobbled walk. His brow was black with anger as the boy and the dog slowly approached.

'You have disobeyed me, Davie Campbell,' he said between tight lips. 'Aye, but what is worse, you have broken the word you gave me.'

Nell Campbell, alerted by the savage clatter of the milk bucket and the harsh voice of her husband, ran swiftly from the house. She bent down and threw her arms protectively around her son.

'You will not strike the lad, Ian,' she said quietly. 'I'll take care of this.'

The big farmer's eyes flashed. 'You will take care of a son who defies his father? A son who breaks his word?' His heavy breathing made his great chest rise and fall, rise and fall. 'I am a patient man, Nell Campbell. But I will not be mocked by my own son.'

'I did what you said,' Davie answered. 'Did I not give you my word?'

'Then what brings the dog back?'

Davie looked at his father, then hesitated. All of a sudden he realized something. How strange his story would sound to the ears of another. It takes faith to pray. It takes a stronger faith to believe that a prayer has been answered. His eyes wavered, then fell. He wet his dry lips with his tongue. He stared fixedly at the smooth cobbles. He did not speak.

'Answer me, boy!' thundered Ian Campbell.

Davie gulped and lifted his head. 'The Angus was not there at all,' he said in a small voice.

'What?'

Even his mother was looking at him queerly. He took a deep breath and went on. 'It's all dried up. There's no more Angus. Joseph—he ran all over where it had been.'

The tight, white lips separated just wide enough to let the words squeeze through. 'And on top of everything else, a liar besides!' His hand shot out and seized Davie roughly by the arm. 'How dare you come to me with such lies! How dare you!'

A stab of pain shot up Davie's arm where the fingers bit cruelly into his flesh.

'It's no lie I tell!' he cried. 'It's the truth! The truth. The Angus is dried up! Would I tell you if it was not so?'

'Aye, it's the truth Davie speaks. I just heard it now. The workmen on the Government project dammed it up. There's a new lake over by Ben Ulva.'

Ian Campbell wheeled round to face the speaker. Murdoch stood quietly and looked at his father. No one spoke for fully a minute.

'A new lake?' Ian Campbell finally said. He looked dazed. Slowly the pain slid from his eyes and down his face. Slowly his fingers gave up their fierce grip on Davie's arm. 'Then the lad did not lie at all?' he asked in a low voice.

'Is he not your son?' Nell Campbell said quietly.

'Aye,' he said slowly, 'he is that.' He seemed lost in thought. 'It will be strange with the Angus gone,' he mused after a pause. He spoke as though to himself. 'Many a grand day's fishing I had there when I was a lad.'

A quick dread chilled Davie's heart. 'I hope you're not minding that the Angus is gone!' he cried anxiously. 'I only asked for a wee miracle. Honest.'

His father was looking at him oddly. So was his mother. So was Murdoch.

'Miracle?' Ian Campbell said. 'You asked for a miracle?'

'Aye. I did. Last night.' He hastened on lest his father would misunderstand. 'But only a wee one. I never dreamed that God would be going to all this bother of drying up rivers.'

'But why, Davie?' It was almost a cry of anguish. 'Why did you want a miracle?'

'It was not for me,' Davie answered hurriedly. 'It was for Joseph.'

'Joseph?' Ian Campbell's face was grey.

Davie nodded. 'Aye, it seemed the only way to save Joseph.' Again he looked quickly at his father. 'But honest, I asked only for a wee miracle.'

For the longest moment Ian Campbell said nothing. And as he stood as though graven in stone, Davie noticed for the first time the streaks of silver in the dark hair. His father's voice when he spoke was soft with a softness Davie had never known.

He smiled a little sadly. 'Aye, Davie. God answers prayers in many ways. After all, does it not say in the Good Book itself that the Lord moves in a mysterious way His wonders to perform?'

Murdoch, who had stood watching the little drama, let a smile flit across his dark face. He ruffled his young brother's red hair. 'Now, Davie,' he said lightly, 'I can understand you having the river dried up and all, but why did you have to start moving mountains around? They must have blasted away half of Ben Ulva when they made that new lake up there.'

Davie stared. Wasn't that the very thing old Tam Menzies said you could do when you had faith? Davie's mind reeled. How was he to have known what mighty forces he would set free last night when he had prayed for Joseph?

Murdoch laughed, then turned to his father.

'They say that the new Government power will be a fine thing for everybody. The electricity will help dry the hay and there will be more fodder for the cattle.' He turned and smiled with his eyes at his young brother. 'And maybe with better times and all we'll be needing some kind of dog around the place.' He scratched his head and looked wryly at Joseph. '*Any* kind of dog.'

Davie's heart skipped a beat. Anxiously he looked at his father. There was no expression on the gaunt face. The dark eyes were fixed on where Joseph lay on the cobbled walk, his chin resting trustingly on the farmer's rough boot.

Slowly Ian Campbell's body relaxed. Slowly he bent down. Slowly he drew a big clumsy finger down Joseph's back. 'Aye,' he said with a soft sigh of resignation, 'maybe it's right you are, Murdoch. Maybe it's right you are.'

The joy in Davie's heart was a winged, soaring thing. Joseph was his! His to keep and to love for ever and ever and ever!

He threw himself down beside his father and never felt the stones that bruised his bare knees. He watched his father. His own wonderful, kind, understanding father. Somehow the sight of him patting the little dog

filled him with a strange and marvellous warmth. And to think that it had only been a few days ago that he had thought he hated this man! Hadn't he been the foolish one! But it was different today. It would *always* be different. Perhaps that was part of the miracle too.

'And it's the great help he'll be to us,' he exulted, 'just wait and see. For it's a grand dog he is with the grand blood in him.' He looked at his father. 'Am I not right?'

Ian Campbell did not smile often. But he smiled now. A smile at once proud and humble. He put out his arm and he pulled his son close to him.

'Aye, the grand blood indeed,' he said.

Dolphin Boy

MARGARET MACKAY

Wiki, the young dolphin, is a lonely orphan. She has lost her mother to a killer whale. So now she swims alone through the waters of Calabash Cove, with only the fishing boats to keep her company. But when she saves Kamuelo from drowning, the Hawaiian boy and the dolphin become firm friends.

Soon all the children from the Cove play happily with Wiki. She clowns and dances and whistles for them, but Kamuelo remains her favourite. They spend hours together, Kamuelo riding on her back through the waves.

But one day Wiki's life is endangered by a giant tidal wave. Kamuelo and his friends must struggle desperately to save her. . . .

Ben's Expedition

GRISELDA GIFFORD

Ben was an Explorer. He'd build a raft and go on a great Expedition. To the sea, why not?

So Ben planned and hammered, and one fine day he set sail. But he didn't get far. And worse, he had to apologise to Colonel Hardy for taking the planks of his fence for the raft. Luckily though, the old Colonel was an Explorer too. So he and Ben set off together – in a punt this time – to discover 'unknown and untrodden lands'. And what marvellous discoveries they made!

THE PADDINGTON BOOKS

MICHAEL BOND

Paddington is a *very* rare bear indeed! He'd travelled all the way from darkest Peru (with only a jar of marmalade, a suitcase and his hat) when the Brown family first met him on Paddington Station. Since then their lives have never been quite the same . . . for things just seem to *happen* to Paddington—chaotic things . . .

What *other* bear could turn his friend's wedding into an uproar by getting the wedding ring stuck on his paw? Or glue himself to his dancing partner's back with his marmalade sandwich? *Only* Paddington . . . but as he says himself, 'Oh dear, I'm in trouble again.'

'Within a comparatively short time, Paddington has joined Pooh as one of the great bears of children's literature.'

The Teacher

Paddington's own particular brand of chaos comes up often in Armada Lions—in *A Bear Called Paddington*, *More About Paddington*, *Paddington Goes to Town*, *Paddington Helps Out*, *Paddington at Large*, *Paddington Abroad*, and *Paddington Takes the Air*.